When The Waterhole Dries Up

Kaye Baillie Max Hamilton

There is a room,
in an outback place,
where a dusty boy is waiting.

And in that room
stands a bath,

a bubbly bath
in an outback place,
where a dusty boy is waiting.

And in that bath creeps a croc,

a clumsy croc
in a bubbly bath
in an outback place,
where a dusty boy is waiting.

And in that bath rushes a roo, a rollicking roo

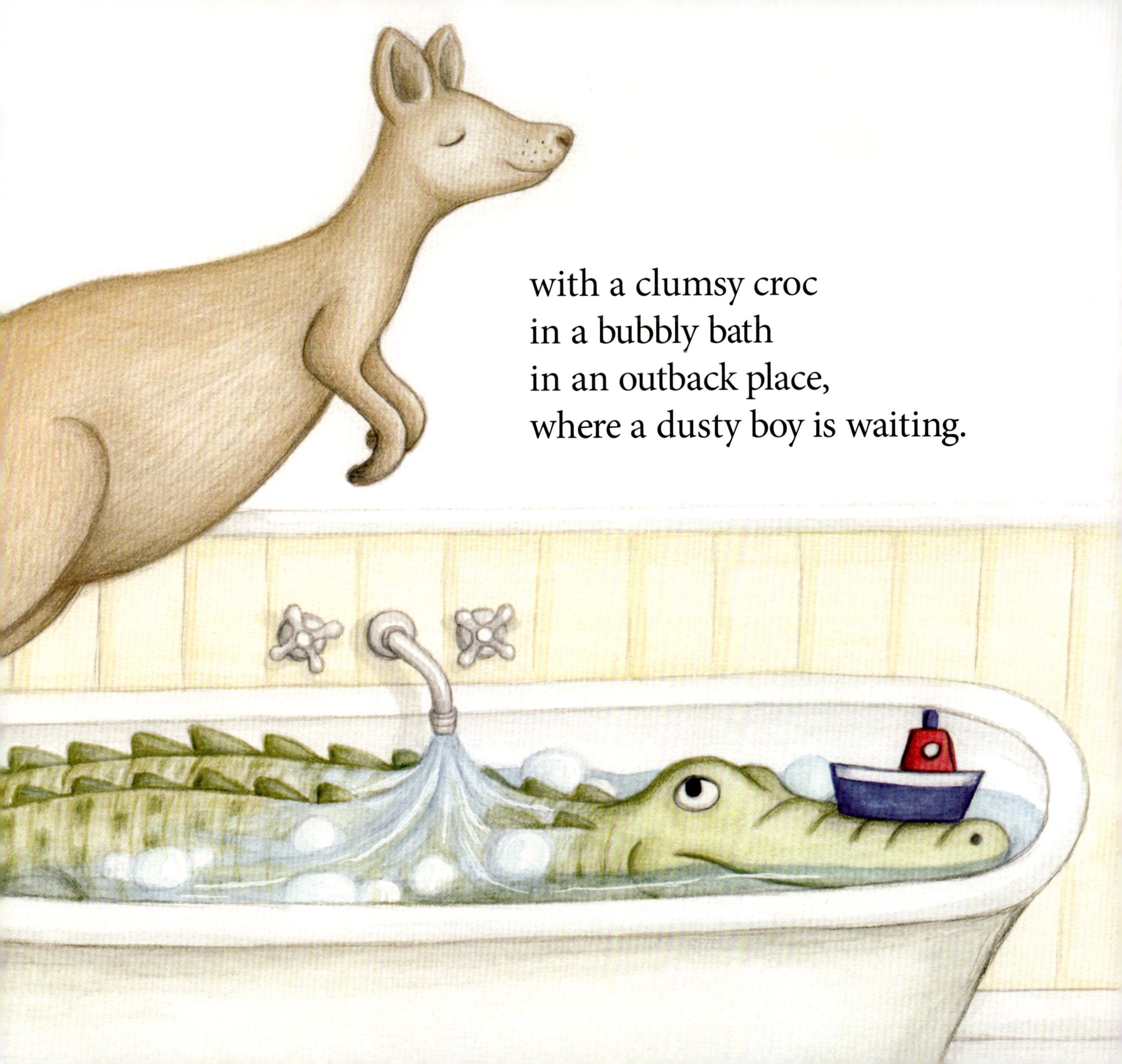

with a clumsy croc
in a bubbly bath
in an outback place,
where a dusty boy is waiting.

And in that bath queues a quoll, a quivering quoll

with a rollicking roo
and a clumsy croc
in a bubbly bath
in an outback place,
where a dusty boy is waiting.

And in that bath
emerges an emu,
an elegant emu

with a quivering quoll and a rollicking roo
and a clumsy croc in a bubbly bath
in an outback place,
where a dusty boy is waiting.

And in that bath
dives a dingo,
a daring dingo

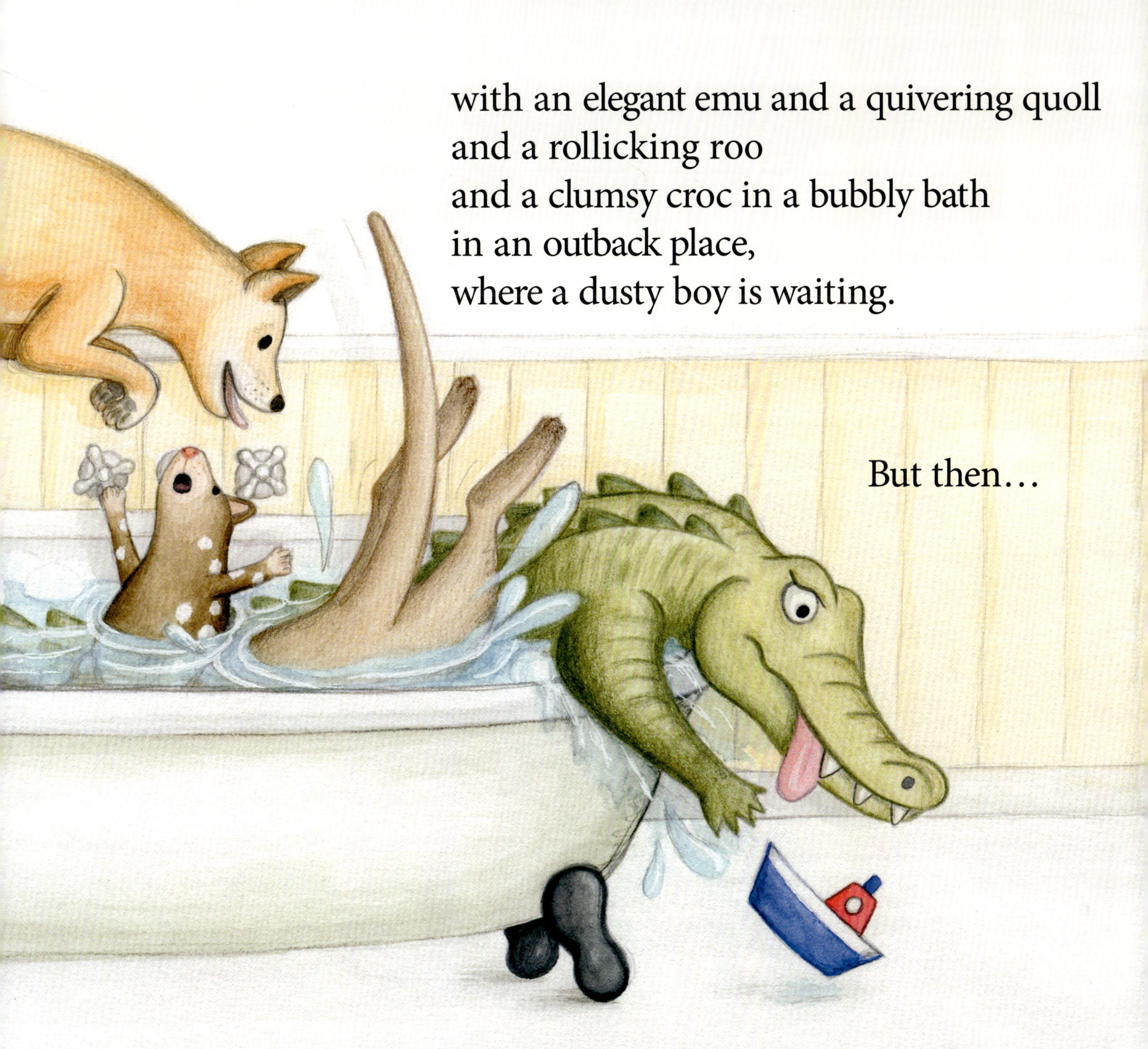

with an elegant emu and a quivering quoll
and a rollicking roo
and a clumsy croc in a bubbly bath
in an outback place,
where a dusty boy is waiting.

But then…

all covered in spikes a dragon appears.

A thorny dragon who likes to dance,
with a daring dingo

and an elegant emu
and a quivering quoll
and a rollicking roo
and a clumsy croc
in a bubbly bath

in an outback place, where a dusty boy is waiting.

The thorny dragon spikes the dingo,

who chases the emu,

who pecks the quoll,

who trips on the roo,

who hops on the croc,

who empties the bath,

in an outback place, where a dusty boy is...

bathing!

For Toad and Albie xx - KB
For Mum and Dad with love - MH

Kaye Baillie grew up writing stories on an orchard with its own waterhole. While she never had to share her bath with animals, she encountered yabbies and leeches while swimming in nearby channels. Kaye is an award winning children's author who swims at the beach in Victoria where she lives with her family.

Max Hamilton is an award winning illustrator, graphic designer and most enthusiastically a maker of children's books. She enjoys noticing the little details in things, loves to get lost in the world of illustration and stories, and through her art aims to raise awareness of the importance of protecting our Australian fauna. Max lives in Sydney with her partner, two young daughters and a couple of guinea pigs named Dumpling and Noodles.

Windy Hollow Books

First published in 2021 by Windy Hollow Books
PO Box 265, Kew East, Victoria, Australia 3102
www.windyhollowbooks.com.au
www.facebook.com/windyhollowbooks

ISBN: 9780645518733 (paperback), 9781922081971 (hardback)

Design by Nuovo Group

A catalogue record for this book is available from the National Library of Australia